Dooty on the Loosey

A.D.A. Hill

illustrated by
Francesco Orazzini

Copyright © 2024 A.D.A Hill

All rights reserved. This book or parts thereof may not be reproduced in any form, stored in any retrieval system, or transmitted in any form by any means—electronic, mechanical, photocopy, recording, or otherwise—without prior written permission of the publisher, except as provided by United States of America copyright law. For permission requests, write to the publisher.

This is a work of fiction. Names, characters, business, events and incidents are the products of the author's imagination. Any resemblance to actual persons, living or dead, or actual events is purely coincidental.

ISBN: 978-1-960157-79-9 (Paperback)
ISBN: 978-1-960157-80-5 (Hardcover)

Dooty on the Loosey

By A.D.A. Hill

1. Fiction

FIRST EDITION

Illustrated by Francesco Orazzini

Published by Bookfox Press

Printed in the United States of America

For Angel.
And to my dear late grandpa, thank you for always believing in me.

Based on a true story

Dooty was a dog who loved her momma.
She'd, in fact, do anything to stay with Momma.

That's when Dooty firmly decided they simply must be reunited.

She plotted away, "The first chance, I'll take! Bert can't stop my great escape!"

Out on a walk that afternoon,
Dooty felt some wiggle room.

She bobbed and weaved and shook her collar.

No one could,

The measures she took were beyond drastic.

For she had one thing on her mind:

"Momma! Momma! I have to find!"

In a nearby park,
Dooty stopped to rest.
She had done her very best.

She sat and howled into the air.
Momma was not anywhere.

Cold and dark the sun was gone.
"At least I have my sweater on."

Dooty said, as she wandered toward the light,
where she saw a big construction site,

"Has anyone seen my momma here?"

"No!"

"No!"

When they said no,
Dooty fought back tears.

Dooty stopped outside a diner
and asked a friendly, dining miner,
"Did you see my momma inside?"

When they said no,
Dooty gave a sigh.

Dooty stopped inside a sauna. "PLEASE, HAS ANYONE SEEN MY MOMMA?!"

"There's a dog in here!" Someone screamed from the corner. Then, suddenly, her run was over!

Dooty was found and taken to Bert.

The very next morning Dooty opened her eyes,
to see her momma, the most pleasant surprise!

Momma had only
been gone for a day,
though to Dooty,
it hadn't seemed that way.

"Momma! Momma,
I knew that you loved me!
Let's go home
and you can rub my tummy."

About the Author

Mother of Angel. Whimsical Artist. Admirer of the Ordinary. Believer in the Extraordinary.

www.ingramcontent.com/pod-product-compliance
Lightning Source LLC
LaVergne TN
LVHW061126291224
800127LV00015B/1056

MR HOWARD THE RESCUED CAT

Written and Illustrated by
Erin Hayburn

Mr Howard the Rescued Cat
Copyright © 2022 by Erin Hayburn

All rights reserved. No part of this publication may be reproduced, distributed, or transmitted in any form or by any means, including photocopying, recording, or other electronic or mechanical methods, without the prior written permission of the author, except in the case of brief quotations embodied in critical reviews and certain other non-commercial uses permitted by copyright law.

Tellwell Talent
www.tellwell.ca

ISBN
978-0-2288-8006-6 (Hardcover)
978-0-2288-8005-9 (Paperback)
978-0-2288-0687-5 (eBook)

For all the unwanted, abandoned, or abused pets
waiting to be rescued, whether it be from
an animal shelter or the streets.

This book will hopefully demonstrate to
all humans, big or small, that with a little love,
(and most certainly a lot of patience), rescuing your
pet will be the most rewarding choice indeed.

They may have had a rough past,
but you can give them a beautiful future.

There once was a young cat with big bushy eyebrows.
He was sad because he had no name.
He had no name because he had no people.

The young cat lived underneath an abandoned house
in a space that was
dark and full of creepy-crawlies.

He had to fend for himself, avoiding the nasty bully cats that roamed the streets at night...

The young cat had not always been alone.
He once had people...

Until one night, the young cat awoke to the sounds of his people rushing out of the house.

They drove off in a hurry with all their possessions...

...except him.
They left him behind.

The young cat waited for his people to return.
Hours became days. Days became weeks.
But still, his people did not come back for him.

The young cat was confused.
He did not understand why his people
had abandoned him.

The young cat was scared.
The young cat was alone...

The young cat was hungry!
He went searching for food under the cover of darkness...but was soon spotted by the nasty bully cats!

The young cat escaped, running back to his abandoned house.
What could he do?
He couldn't find food. The nasty bully cats were fearsome and never let the young cat roam.
He needed help...

Then one day, the young cat saw new people looking over the fence of the abandoned house...
They were looking at him.

These new people seemed concerned about him.

They looked over the fence each day, checking to see if he was still alone, checking if he had any food or water.
They spoke softly to him, telling him everything would be ok...

Then the new people brought around bowls of food and water for him…

But the young cat was scared of the strangers.
His last people had abandoned him.
Could he trust these new people?

The young cat's stomach rumbled; he was so hungry!
He couldn't resist anymore! He cautiously
approached the food and water bowls...
Was it a trap? Was it poison?

He sniffed the bowls...
They smelt good...

He tentatively tested
the water...
Cool and fresh. Not poison...

He nibbled the food...
Delicious. Not poison...

Did these new people want to help him?

Over the next few weeks, the new people patiently
fed the young cat, and he very slowly came to trust them.
Each day he let them come closer and closer...

Eventually, the young cat let the new people carry
him home with them...

The new people wanted to give the young cat a name.

They believed the first name that pops into your head is often the right one.
The young cat's fluffy features and big bushy eyebrows made them instantly think he looked like a Mr Howard.

The young cat was very proud of his new name.
It sounded quite posh indeed!

Mr Howard had been rescued.
He had a name and new people.
He was ready to start his new life...

However, Mr Howard was not used to having a nice home.
He was not used to being locked inside.
He most certainly was not used to RULES!
Needless to say, Mr Howard was a little naughty
when he first arrived at his new home – with the
shredded furniture copping the worst of it!

So, Mr Howard's new people gave him
his very own scratching pole!
He would scratch this pole when he thought about
doing something he knew he should not...or
when he got caught doing something he should not...

Mr Howard's new home came with
a little dog called Old Girl.

A very fitting name, Mr Howard thought,
as the dog looked quite ancient to him.
Her eyes were white with blindness.
She was small, frail, and undeniably a bit deaf.
Her potbelly showed she was well fed.
Her old age was proof of a good life in this home.

RULE NUMBER 1 was to never hurt Old Girl.

Mr Howard didn't understand that the way he played, as a sprightly young cat, may be a little too rough for a very old, very brittle, small dog. He hid, waiting for Old Girl to waddle past, unsuspecting...

He twitched with excitement, ready to pounce...
Just as he was about to leap out...
"*Oi!*" one of the new people exclaimed. Busted!
Mr Howard ran from the scene quick smart!
Old Girl continued to waddle along, none the wiser.

Mr Howard *was* allowed to cuddle with Old Girl.

He enjoyed snuggling up to Old Girl each night.
She made him feel safe and warm.

RULE NUMBER 2 was to never go outside.

The new people loved all animals.
They knew if Mr Howard returned outside,
his natural instincts to hunt innocent creatures
would come back to him.

Mr Howard was not a fan of this RULE.
He wondered how he was going to entertain himself
if he couldn't go outside...

But the new people gave Mr Howard lots of toys!
His favourite toy was his green rabbit.
It was soft and cuddly.

He loved playing with his new toys.
They were lots of fun and kept him entertained.

The new people even gave him a soft bed to sleep in! Mr Howard felt like he was sleeping on a marshmallow cloud, especially when he remembered the hard, cold ground he used to sleep on!

RULE NUMBER 3 was to not scratch the furniture.

This RULE was broken quite regularly...

RULE NUMBER 4 was to get brushed every day.

Mr Howard had never been brushed before.
He was not pleased with this RULE.
However, with time and a lot of patience,
Mr Howard allowed his new people to brush him…

He noticed how much nicer his fur looked and felt.
He was smooth and shiny.
It made him feel amazing and very handsome indeed.

Mr Howard asked Old Girl why the new people wanted to keep him.

He was from the street. He had a rough past.
He had learnt that he could not always trust humans.

Old Girl said she too had been rescued by these people many years ago.
She had been rescued from a pound.

Old Girl had once been treated very unkindly by humans. Like Mr Howard, she had also been abandoned…

But the new people had rescued her.
They had given her a second chance at life.

Not all humans are bad, Old Girl explained.
Many of them love animals and want to help or rescue those who need it most.
Those like Old Girl. Those like Mr Howard.

Mr Howard was slowly settling into his new home.
He was obeying the RULES (most of the time).

But one day, something happened...

Despite **RULE NUMBER 2**, Mr Howard escaped
through an open door!

He ran outside, out into the wild, out to freedom!!!

Mr Howard hid, chuckling to himself, impressed with his escape.

No more RULES to follow!

He was free to hunt and scratch whatever he wanted!
He would certainly never need to get brushed again!

...Although, he actually quite liked getting brushed.
It felt good. It made him look good.

...Although, he would not get fed every day out here.
He'd have to find his own food, braving the streets
and the nasty bully cats…

...Although, he would not get to curl up in his
warm cosy bed. He would be back to sleeping
on the hard, cold ground…

…Who would look after his toys while he was gone?
Oh no, Old Girl might take them!

…He would miss snuggling with Old Girl.
She might even miss his warm cuddles too.

…Maybe the RULES were not so bad
when they came with so much good.

…He had even started to feel like the new people
were not just new people. They were his new
family…

He knew they cared about him. They had given him
so much love, patience, toys, and food.
He knew they would be worried about him.
They would be worried he might get hurt by
the nasty bully cats or hit by a car.
They would be worried he may never
come back to them…

Mr Howard had a choice:

Did he want to go back to his old life on the streets,
where he was scared, hungry, and alone?

Or did he want to go back to the people who had
rescued him? Fed him? Cared for him?

It was not a hard choice in the end.
Mr Howard ran back to his new people.
He meowed at the door – "I'm back!!!"

The new people instantly let him in.
His people. His family.

Mr Howard purred loudly like a motor.
He was happy. He was home.

Mr Howard had been rescued.

www.ingramcontent.com/pod-product-compliance
Lightning Source LLC
LaVergne TN
LVHW061126291224
800127LV00015B/1057